Muncha! Muncha! Muncha!

by
Candace Fleming

Illustrated by
G. Brian Karas

SIMON & SCHUSTER, LONDON

For Martha and Dan
— G. B. K.

To my muncha-muncha-
munching boys,
Scott and Michael
— C. F.

SIMON &
SCHUSTER

First published in Great Britain in 2002
by Simon & Schuster UK Ltd
Africa House, 64-78 Kingsway,
London WC2B 6AH

Text copyright © 2002 by Candace Fleming
Illustrations copyright © 2002 by G. Brian Karas

For years, Mr McGreely dreamed of planting a garden. He dreamed of getting his hands dirty, of growing yummy vegetables, and of gobbling them all up.

But he never tried it until —

"This spring!" said Mr McGreely. "This spring, by golly, I'm going to plant a garden."

So he hoed.

And he sowed.

And he watched his garden grow.

Lettuce!   Carrots!   Peas!   Tomatoes!
"Yum! Yum! Yummy!" said Mr McGreely. "I'll soon
fill my tummy with crisp, fresh veggies."

But one night, when the sun went down and the moon came up, three hungry bunnies appeared.

Tippy —

Tippy —

Tippy,

Pat!

Muncha!

Muncha!

Muncha!

The next morning, when Mr McGreely saw his gnawed sprouts,
he was angry.
    So he built a small wire fence
        all around his vegetable garden.

"There," he declared. "No bunny can get into my garden now!"

And the sun went down.
And the moon came up. And —

Tippy-tippy-
tippy,
Pat!

Spring-hurdle,
Dash! Dash! Dash!

Muncha!

Muncha!

Muncha!

The next morning, when Mr McGreely saw his nibbled leaves
and gnawed sprouts, he was really angry.
    So he built a tall wooden wall
        behind the small wire fence
        all around his vegetable garden.
    "Hmpf!" he huffed.
"Those flop-ears will
never get over it.
No bunny can get into
my garden now."

And the sun went down.
And the moon came up. And —

Tippy-
tippy-
tippy,
Pat!

Dig-scrabble,
Scratch! Scratch!
Scratch!

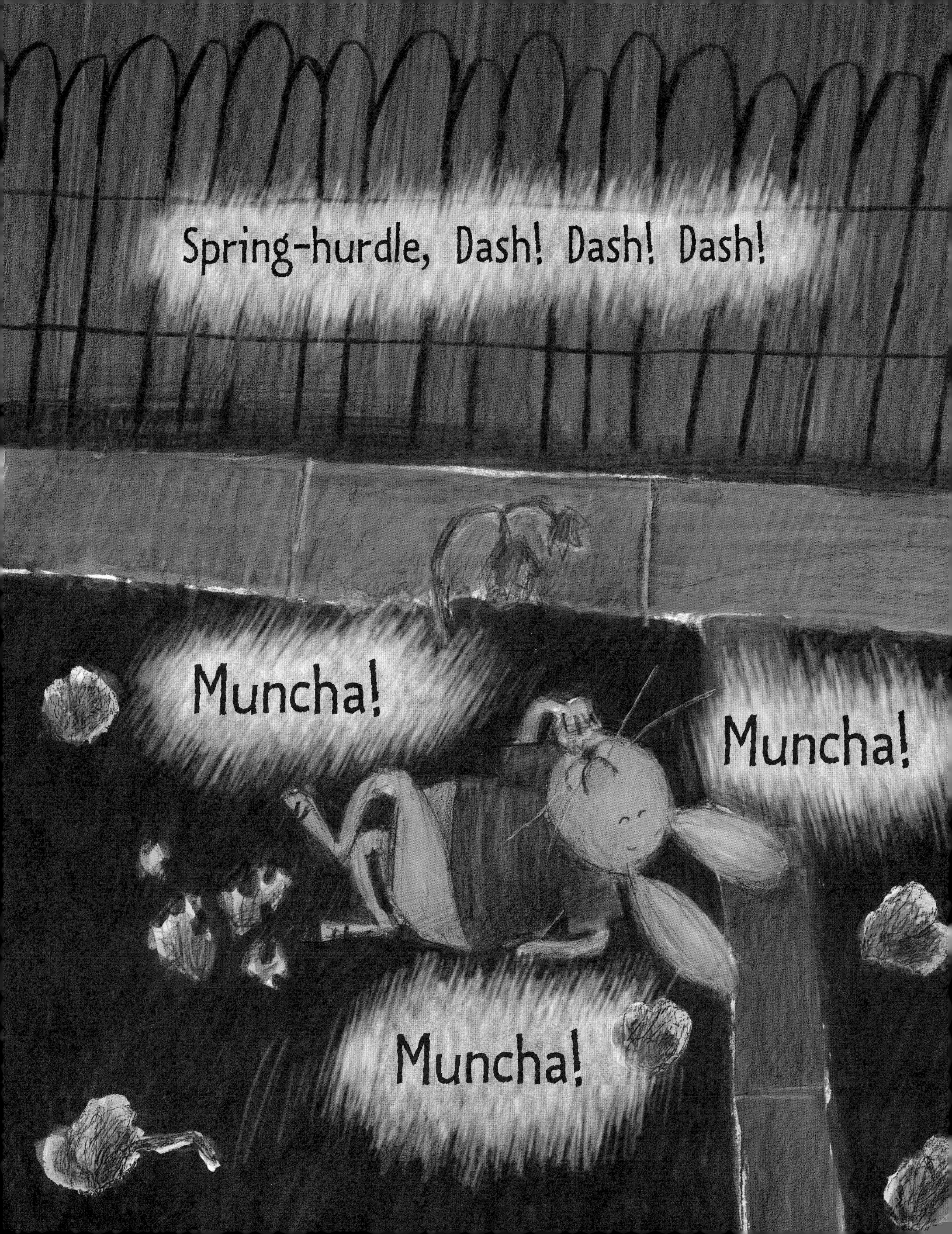
Spring-hurdle, Dash! Dash! Dash!
Muncha!
Muncha!
Muncha!

The next morning, when Mr McGreely saw his chewed stems, his nibbled leaves, and his gnawed sprouts,

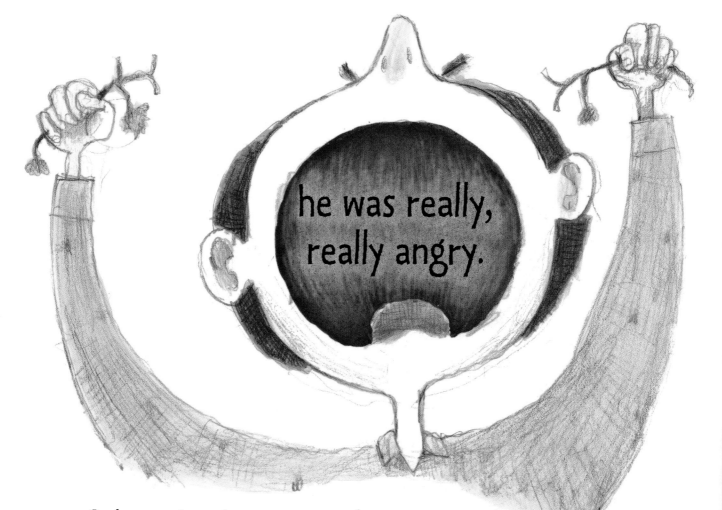

he was really, really angry.

So he made a deep wet trench,
    outside the tall wooden wall
    behind the small wire fence
    all around his vegetable garden.
"Hah!" he snorted. "Those puff-tails can't get under it. They can't get over it. No bunny can get into my garden now!"

And the sun went down. And the moon came up. And —

Tippy-tippy-
tippy,
Pat!

Dive-paddle,
Splash!
Splash!
Splash!

Dig-scrabble, Scratch! Scratch!
Scratch!

Spring-hurdle,
Dash! Dash! Dash!

Muncha!

Muncha!

Muncha!

The next morning, when Mr McGreely saw his chomped blossoms,
his chewed stems, his nibbled leaves, and his gnawed sprouts, he was —

FURIOUS!

So he hammered and blocked, sawed and stocked,
drilled and filled, and trapped and locked.
And he built a huge, enormous thing
   before the deep wet trench
   outside the tall wooden wall
   behind the small wire fence
   all around his vegetable garden.
"I've outsmarted those twitch-whiskers for sure,"
he exclaimed. "They can't get through it. They can't
get under it. And they can't get over it. No bunny, no
way, no how, can get into my vegetable garden now!"

And the sun went down.

And the moon came up. And —

Tippy-tippy-tippy, STOP!

The three hungry bunnies looked and smelled and touched the huge, enormous thing before them. And —

Tippy-tippy-tippy, pat.

The bunnies hopped away.

The next morning, when Mr McGreely
saw his untouched vegetables, he was —

happy!

"I beat the bunnies!"
he whooped, and did
a jiggly, wiggly
victory dance.
Then he —

climbed over,

jumped across,

squeezed between,

and crawled under until he reached his vegetable garden.
"Ahh!" sighed Mr McGreely. "At last!" Smacking his lips, he picked
and pulled up Lettuce! Carrots! Peas! Tomatoes! And when his
basket was overflowing, he reached inside for something yummy.

Muncha!

Muncha!

Muncha!